Berni Bakes a Cake

Susie Wunderli Clark

Illustrations by
Laura Jeanne

Fulton Books, Inc.
Meadville, PA

Published by Fulton Books 2021

ISBN 978-1-6371-0143-8 (paperback)
ISBN 978-1-63860-238-5 (hardcover)
ISBN 978-1-6371-0144-5 (digital)

Printed in the United States of America

Berni wants to do something
nice for her dad.
She decides to bake a cake
to make him feel glad.

4

She gets a bowl, a pan, a
spoon, and egg beaters.

She must follow the
recipe; there's no
room for cheaters.

Chocolate Cake
3 C. Flour
3 C. Sugar
1½ C. Cocoa
4 eggs
1½ C. milk
1 t. baking soda

Preheat oven 350°

She adds eggs, butter,
sugar, and flour.

Berni says to herself, "This
will take about an hour."

60
50
40

1   10   20   30

"We must plug in the mixer,"
she says to her mom.

"Dad's going to love this. He'll think it's the BOMB!"

10

She's on a roll now; there's
no need to fuss.

Her dad will simply say,
"This is just fabulous!"

Now Berni's eyesight is not very great.

But wearing eyeglasses is
the thing she does hate!

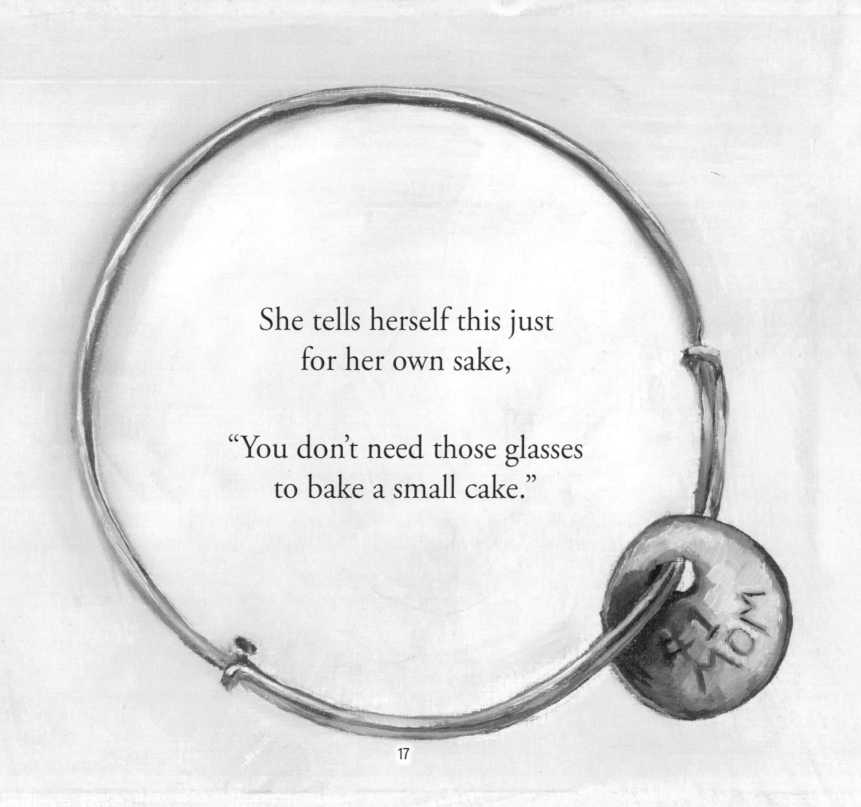

She tells herself this just
for her own sake,

"You don't need those glasses
to bake a small cake."

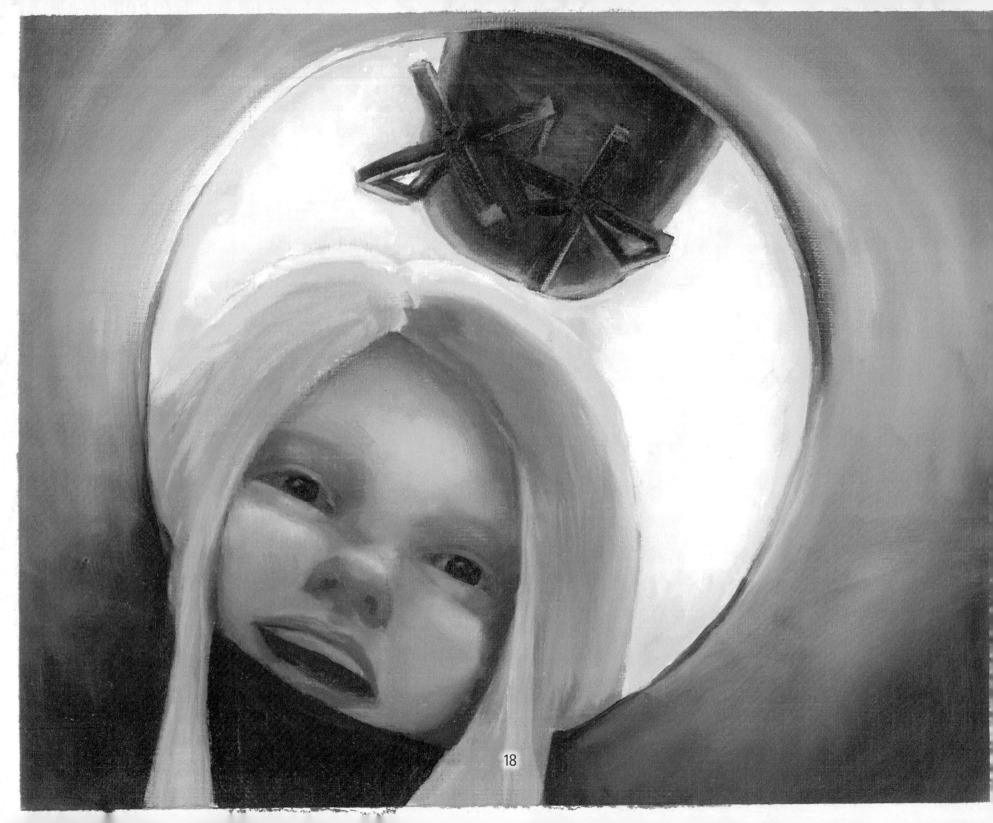

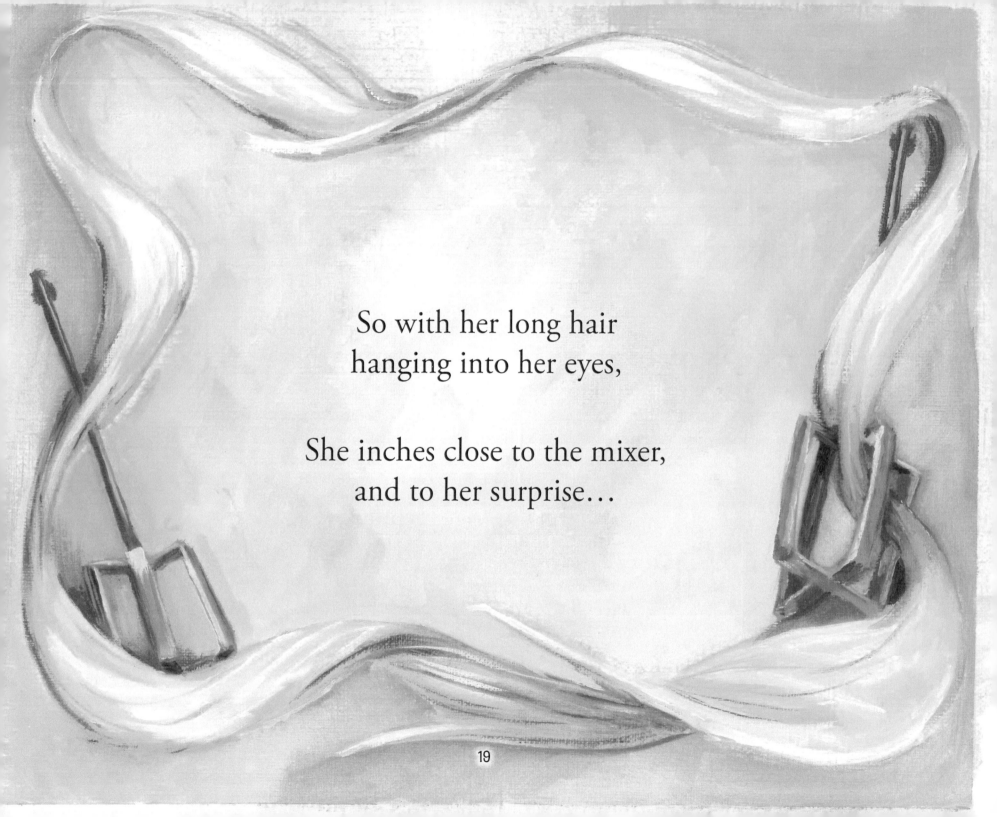

So with her long hair
hanging into her eyes,

She inches close to the mixer,
and to her surprise…

The mixer, it seems, has
a talent for flair.

Its beaters have rolled up
into her long hair.

21

With batter and tears dripping
down her sweet face,
Her mom helps her unplug,
unwind, and erase.

22

So with a small kiss and
a muffled laugh,

Her mom helps her jump
into a warm bath.

Now clean and refreshed,
she's a girl on a mission.

Those beaters won't change
her lofty ambition.

27

Except maybe this time, she'll
wear her eyeglasses

To mix up the batter she'll
feed to the masses.

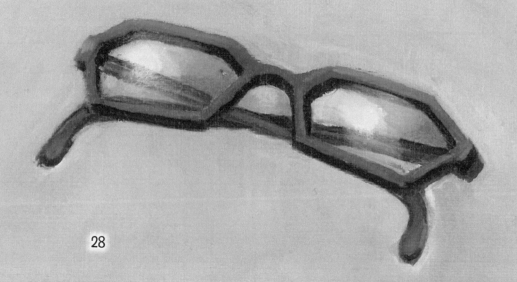

She bakes that small cake
and cuts a slice for her
dad.

30

And with only three
hairs in his slice…

He is glad.

About the Author

Susie Wunderli Clark lives in the mountains of Utah where she and her husband raised their five children. Susie loves adventure, lives colorfully, and laughs a lot. She is happiest in the mountains, in a lake, or by the ocean and believes life is best enjoyed through humor and love. *Berni Bakes a Cake* is Susie's first children's book.

About the Illustrator

Laura Jeanne is an artist of the classical atelier tradition. She has always had a love for children and believes it is the appreciation of each child's light that brings her drawings and paintings of them to life. There is magic in the world when you look through a child's eyes; things to still be awed by and endless horizons to explore. This remembered perspective is what allows her art to illuminate the heart and mind of the observer.